復於過去無量阿僧祇劫有佛出世名清淨蓮華目如來其佛壽命四十劫像法之中一羅漢福度眾生因次教化遇一女人字曰光目設食供養羅漢問之欲願何等光目答言我以母亡之日資福救拔未知我母生處何趣羅漢愍之為入定觀見光目女母墮在惡趣受極大苦羅漢問光目言汝母在生作何行業今在惡趣受極大苦光目答言我母所習唯好食噉魚鱉之屬所食魚鱉多食其子或炒或煮恣情食噉計其命數千萬復倍尊者慈愍如何哀救羅漢愍之為作方便勸光目言汝可志誠念清淨蓮華目如來兼塑畫形像存亡獲報光目聞已即捨所愛尋畫佛像而供養之復恭敬心悲泣瞻禮忽於夜後夢見佛身金色晃耀如須彌山放大光明而告光目汝母不久當生汝家纔覺飢寒即當言說其後家內婢生一子未滿三日而乃言說稽首悲泣告於光目生死業緣果報自受吾是汝母久處暗冥自別汝來累墮大地獄蒙汝福力方得受生為下賤人又復短命壽年十三更落惡道汝有何計令吾脫免光目聞說知母無疑哽咽悲啼而白婢子既是我母合知本罪作何行業墮於惡道婢子答言以殺害毀罵二業受報若非蒙福救拔吾難以是業故未合解脫光目問言地獄罪報其事云何婢子答言罪苦之事不忍稱說百千歲中卒白難竟光目聞已啼淚號泣而白空界願我之母永脫地獄畢十三歲更無重罪及歷惡道十方諸佛慈哀愍我聽我為母所發廣大誓願若得我母永離三塗及斯下賤乃至女人之身永劫不受者願我今日後對清淨蓮華目如來像前卻後百千萬億劫中應有世界所有地獄及三惡道諸罪苦眾生誓願救拔令離地獄惡趣畜生餓鬼等如是罪報等人盡成佛竟我然後方成正覺發誓願已具聞清淨蓮華目如來而告之日光目汝大慈愍善能為母發如是大願吾觀汝母十三歲畢捨此報已生為梵志壽年百歲過是報後當生無憂國土壽命不可計劫後成佛果廣度人天數如恆河沙佛告定自在王爾時羅漢福度光目者即無盡意菩薩是光目母者即解脫菩薩是光目女者即地藏菩薩是過去久遠劫中如是慈愍發恆河沙願廣度眾生。

天地圖書
香港大學佛學研究中心
共同出版

澳門佛教青年中心
支持

光目救母
Guang Mu Saving her Mother

文 / 王冰　　圖 / Kin Tai

很久很久以前，有一位名叫光目的女子。
她心地善良，沉靜可愛。

光目是虔誠的佛教徒，她有一個心願，就是希望自己早日成佛。
光目每日在家中拜佛，也常常念誦佛的名號「清淨蓮華目如來」。
多好聽的名字啊！每當念誦時，光目的心裏都很歡喜。

有一天，光目遇見一位雲遊四方的阿羅漢。

阿羅漢是誰呢？原來是人們對有所成就的修行者的稱呼。

阿羅漢認真修行，平日以托缽乞食為生。不論是誰送來的食物，

也不論食物是否美味，阿羅漢都會感恩地享用。

光目十分恭敬地準備食物，供奉給這位阿羅漢。

光目相信阿羅漢能夠看到人的前世今生，她想起已經過世的母親。
光目一直思念母親，她很想知道母親下一世會投生到甚麼地方去，
於是請求阿羅漢告訴她。

9

阿羅漢被光目的一片孝心感動，決定幫助她實現這一心願。
只見阿羅漢盤膝靜坐，心神專注，在一片寧靜中看到光目的母親
墮落在地獄道裏，正承受着極大的苦痛。

為甚麼會這樣呢？

原來光目的母親在世時，最喜歡吃魚鱉海鮮，常常任意宰殺活魚，將魚的腹部剖開，取出魚子來煮食。魚媽媽的腹中有成千上萬的魚子，光目的母親因此傷害了無數生命，死後墮落在地獄道中。

光目知道母親正在地獄道中受苦，非常難過。

她流着淚問道：「慈悲的阿羅漢，請問您是否能告訴我解救母親的方法。哪怕赴湯蹈火，我也心甘情願。」

每個人都要為自己的行為負責，也必須承擔因此而產生的後果……
光目用甚麼方法才能解救母親呢？
阿羅漢沉思片刻，對光目說道：「你不妨試試看，以虔誠的心來念誦
清淨蓮華目如來的名號，還可以恭敬地描摹塑畫佛的形象，
用這樣的方式淨化身心，為母親所犯下的罪過懺悔，為她祈福吧。
你的孝心也許能感動天地萬物呢！」

「好的，我一定這樣做！希望救母親脫離苦海。」
於是，光目變賣家產，四處邀請能工巧匠和畫師，為佛塑像和畫像，
她自己則日夜虔誠念誦清淨蓮華目如來的名號，一心一意為母親祈福。

有一天晚上，光目夢見了清淨蓮華目如來。佛的身體放射出溫暖又明亮的光芒。清淨蓮華目如來告訴光目，
她的母親不久之後便能離開地獄了，
還會再次轉世投生到她家中。

果然，不久後，
光目家有一位女傭人生下一個孩子。

這小嬰兒出生不到三天，就能開口說話，大家都覺得驚奇。
小嬰兒一見到光目，就傷心地流下眼淚。她對光目說：
「我就是你死去的母親轉世啊。以前所做的種種惡業，都要自作自受。
自從與你離別後，我一直在地獄中受各種各樣的苦。多虧你日夜念佛，
我才能再次投生到人間。但是因為我的罪業深重，
這一生也只能活到十三歲，死後還要再次墮入地獄受苦。
真不知道怎樣才能得到徹底的解脫啊！」

光目聽到這番話，知道小嬰兒正是母親的轉世，她又傷心又歡喜。
為了令母親能永遠脫離地獄道之苦，光目再次發下一個大願：
「從今以後，我要幫助一切在惡道中受苦難的眾生，
直到他們全部得到解脫，我才能夠成佛。」

正是因為光目立下了這樣一個慈悲的大願，
她的母親得到救度。後來亦勤奮地學習佛法，認真修行，
最終也修成正果。

這位有着大慈悲的光目女是誰呢？
原來她就是地藏菩薩的前世啊！

A long time ago, there was a girl named Guang Mu (meaning bright-eyed). She was kind-hearted, quiet and sweet.

*   *   *

Guang Mu was a devout Buddhist dedicated to the early accomplishment of Buddhahood. She made daily prostrations in veneration of the Buddha, often reciting the Buddha's name "Pure Lotus Eye Tathagata". What a wonderful name! Whenever Guang Mu chanted that name, she would be filled with joy.

*   *   *

One day, Guang Mu met a travelling Arhat. Who is an Arhat? We call someone who is accomplished in cultivation an Arhat. An Arhat is a mendicant who takes his cultivation very seriously and would go on his daily alms-round begging for food. An Arhat would accept with gratitude whatever food is given to him regardless of whether it tastes good or bad.

With deep respect, Guang Mu prepared some food as an offering to the Arhat.

*   *   *

Believing that an Arhat could see one's past and present lives, Guang Mu thought of her late mother. Missing her mother very much and wondering where she was reborn, Guang Mu implored the Arhat to tell her where was her mother.

*   *   *

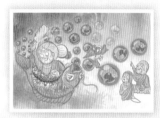

Moved by Guang Mu's filial love for her mother, the Arhat decided to fulfil her wish. Sitting down with crossed legs in the lotus position, the Arhat gathered his concentration to focus his mind. In a state of tranquil quietude, he observed that Guang Mu's mother had fallen into hell and was in great suffering.

*   *   *

Why would that be? It is because when Guang Mu's mother was alive, she loved to eat seafood such as fish and turtle, and would often slit open the bellies of fishes that were still alive to get their roe for cooking. As a mother fish would have thousands of these roe in her belly, it means Guang Mu's mother had harmed and killed countless lives and therefore fallen into hell when she died.

*   *   *

On hearing that her mother was suffering in hell, Guang Mu became very sad and asked the Arhat in tears: "Compassionate one, please tell me if there's a way to save my mother. I'm ready to face any danger even if it means having to risk my own life."

*   *   *

A person must be responsible for his or her actions and ready to bear the consequences. What action must Guang Mu take to save her mother?

The Arhat pondered for a while before answering Guang Mu: "Perhaps you can try to devoutly recite the name of Pure Lotus Eye Tathagata

and respectfully make paintings or images of the Buddha. This would purify your body and mind so you can repent for your mother's past misdeeds and invoke blessings for her. Heaven and earth might be touched by such a filial act of yours."

*　　*　　*

"Alright, I'll do as you say and hope this would help to deliver my mother from her sufferings!" Thereafter, Guang Mu sold all her possessions and looked everywhere for artisans and painters to make images and paintings of the Buddha. As for herself, she devoted all her time to invoking blessings for her mother by reciting the name of Pure Lotus Eye Tathagata.

*　　*　　*

One night, Guang Mu saw Pure Lotus Eye Tathagata in her dream. The Buddha's body emitted such a warm and brilliant radiance that she could hardly look directly at the Buddha. Pure Lotus Eye Tathagata told Guang Mu that her mother would soon leave hell and be reborn into her household.

*　　*　　*

Indeed, not long afterwards, a maid working in the household of Guang Mu gave birth to a child.

*　　*　　*

When the newborn child opened her mouth to speak at just three days' old, everyone was amazed. On seeing Guang Mu for the first time,

the child broke down in tears and said to her: "I'm your late mother now reborn. I have to bear the consequences of all my past evil deeds. Ever since we parted, I've been suffering in all sorts of ways in hell. It is only thanks to your daily recitation of the Buddha's name that I'm once again reborn into this human world. However, due to the heavy burden of karma from my past misdeeds, I can only live to thirteen years of age and thereafter return to hell for further sufferings. I really don't know when I could be completely emancipated!"

*　　*　　*

On hearing this, Guang Mu knew that the child was her late mother, and she was at the same time both delighted and sad.

In order to forever rid her mother of the sufferings in hell, Guang Mu once again made a vow: "I shall henceforth help to deliver suffering beings in the evil paths, and not until all of them are emancipated would I become a Buddha."

*　　*　　*

As a result of Guang Mu's great vow of compassion, her mother was eventually delivered. Guang Mu continued to diligently study and practice Buddhist teachings until she finally attained the fruit of Buddhahood.

*　　*　　*

Who was this compassionate girl Guang Mu? She was in fact Ksitigarbha Bodhisattva in a past life.

後記

這套小書即將陸續出版，要感謝很多人。首先是衍空法師，因為他的引介，數年前我得以與澳門佛教青年中心的盧婉君居士相識，因此有機緣參與這個有關《地藏經》的研究計劃；還有研究計劃的總負責人、導師廣興副教授，感謝他的信任，將項目其中一個成果——即這套繪本系列的策劃與執行全權交托，給我空間進行各種努力與嘗試，這其中有失敗有挫折，也有感動與歡喜，特別感謝行政同事Amy在背後提供有力的行政支援；還有天地圖書陳儉雯女士，為我們提供出版的一切便利，促成是次香港大學佛學研究中心與天地圖書共同出版繪本系列的契機。

繪本是以簡單圖文呈現豐富內容與想像的一種形式，想做得好非常不易。在這個學習的過程中，要接受個人的局限，也要面對因緣條件的無常與變化。所幸一路走來，我得到幾位出版界與繪本界前輩毫無保留的指導。資深出版人、編輯汪家明先生，前日本福音館編輯、繪本作家與譯者唐亞明先生為繪本文字逐字修訂。有時一個字或一個標點符號的變更，便令到整句話呈現不同的風貌。愚鈍如我者，在前輩們的提攜之下，也有微小進步。老一輩人謙謙君子之風、儒雅溫煦又嚴謹的態度，是潛移默化的養份，感動之餘，亦令我常自反省，獲益良多。

曾擔任臺灣新竹教育大學藝術與設計系教授的徐素霞女士，是第一位入選意大利波隆那插畫展的台灣畫家（1989年），曾參與創作很多繪本。在研究領域，徐教授非常重視圖畫書的圖像特質與藝術表現力，她目光銳利，在每一輪修訂中都會直擊問題所在，提供最中肯的意見。直到繪本送印前的最後一分鐘，我們還在探討一些文字與圖畫細節仍然有可提升的空間；香港大學佛學研究中心佛教藝術專家崔中慧博士是相識多年、亦師亦友的善知識，她專工佛教藝術，為繪本系列提供很多可參考的佛教與圖像資料。譯者何蕙儀女士是一位身體力行的佛教修行者，她慈悲應允為本書做英譯，令英文讀者也有因緣得以閱讀。

有人會說，不過是幾行文字，數幀圖畫，有必要如此大費周章嗎？是的，有必要。透過「大願地藏繪本系列」，我們嘗試以現代大眾更易接受、更年輕化的形式來探索佛教經典中的普世價值於當今社會層面的應用，希望令佛教中的經典故事為更多人所了解，及進一步創作與主題相關的現代原創故事。同時，可以藉此鼓勵更多優秀的繪本作者與畫家參與到佛教繪本的創作中來。這也正是捐助方澳門佛教青年中心以及香港大學佛學研究中心將繪本系列納入研究計劃的初衷。

要感謝的人還有很多很多，無法一一盡述。我相信，是地藏菩薩的感召力，讓每一位參與這項目的人得以與這套小書結緣。透過這個繪本系列，我們希望能夠將地藏菩薩的大願和慈悲精神傳遞給每一位讀者。

王冰
2021年6月

謹以此繪本系列緬懷已故澳門佛教青年中心創始人暢懷長老。

「大願地藏繪本系列」為《地藏菩薩本願經》研究計劃成果之一，計劃的研究工作由香港大學佛學研究中心主持，澳門佛教青年中心贊助。

顧問委員會
釋衍空、釋演慈、李焯芬、盧婉君、馬淑娟

計劃負責人
廣興

計劃統籌
王冰

特別鳴謝
為繪本系列提供編輯、文字以及圖畫指導的特邀專家顧問，包括資深出版人汪家明先生，前日本福音館編輯、繪本作家與譯者唐亞明先生，臺灣新竹教育大學藝術與設計系教授、兒童繪本作家徐素霞女士，香港大學佛學研究中心佛教藝術專家崔中慧博士。

www.cosmosbooks.com.hk

書　　名	光目救母	
策　　劃	香港大學佛學研究中心	
主編/文字	王冰	
圖　　畫	Kin Tai	
英　　譯	何蕙儀	
責任編輯	王穎嫻	
美術編輯	郭志民	

出　　版　　天地圖書有限公司　香港大學佛學研究中心
　　　　　　香港黃竹坑道46號新興工業大廈11樓（總寫字樓）
　　　　　　電話：2528 3671　傳真：2865 2609

　　　　　　香港灣仔莊士敦道30號地庫（門市部）
　　　　　　電話：2865 0708　傳真：2861 1541

印　　刷　　亨泰印刷有限公司
　　　　　　柴灣利眾街27號德景工業大廈10字樓
　　　　　　電話：2896 3687　傳真：2558 1902

發　　行　　香港聯合書刊物流有限公司
　　　　　　香港新界荃灣德士古道220-248號荃灣工業中心16樓
　　　　　　電話：2150 2100　傳真：2407 3062

出版日期　　2021年7月初版‧香港

本書文字版稅收益悉數撥捐予文教慈善用途。